DISNEY
PRINCESS

5-
Minute
Horse
Stories

DISNEY PRESS
Los Angeles • New York

"Merida's Wild Ride" written by Susan Amerikaner. Copyright © 2013 Disney Enterprises, Inc. Originally published in *Scary Storybook Collection*. Copyright © 2017 Disney Enterprises, Inc.

"Princess Polo Games" written by Kitty Richards. Copyright © 2018 Disney Enterprises, Inc. Originally published in *5-Minute Girl Power Stories*. Copyright © 2020 Disney Enterprises, Inc.

"The Enchanted Unicorn Adventure" written by Aubre Andrus. Copyright © 2020 Disney Enterprises, Inc.

"Snow White's Forest Journey" adapted from "To the Rescue," written by Laura Driscoll and originally published in *Enchanted Stables*. Copyright © 2007 Disney Enterprises, Inc.

"Aurora and the Joust" adapted from "An Amazing Team," written by Tea Orsi. Copyright © 2019 Disney Enterprises, Inc. Originally published in *5-Minute Girl Power Stories*. Copyright © 2020 Disney Enterprises, Inc.

"Bedtime for Max" written by Rebecca Schmidt. Copyright © 2016 Disney Enterprises, Inc. Originally published in *Princess Bedtime Stories*. Copyright © 2017 Disney Enterprises, Inc.

"Against All Odds" adapted by Elizabeth Rudnick from "The Desert Race," written by Catherine Hapka and originally published in *Royal Champions*. Copyright © 2008 Disney Enterprises, Inc.

"The Perfect Team" adapted by Elizabeth Rudnick from "Buttercup the Brave," written by Catherine Hapka and originally published in *Royal Champions*. Copyright © 2008 Disney Enterprises, Inc.

"Heart of a Champion" adapted from the story written by Lara Bergen and originally published in *Enchanted Stables*. Copyright © 2007 Disney Enterprises, Inc.

"A Friend for Philippe" written by Lara Bergen and originally published in *Enchanted Stables*. Copyright © 2007 Disney Enterprises, Inc.

"Khan to the Rescue" written by Calliope Glass. Copyright © 2016 Disney Enterprises, Inc.

"Merida's Winning Friendship" written by John Edwards. Copyright © 2019 Disney Enterprises, Inc.

All illustrations by the Disney Storybook Art Team.

For information address Disney Press, 1200 Grand Central Avenue, Glendale, California 91201.

Printed in the United States of America

First Hardcover Edition, June 2022

Library of Congress Control Number: 2021949825

1 3 5 7 9 10 8 6 4 2

ISBN 978-1-368-07677-7

FAC-034274-22112

For more Disney Press fun, visit www.disneybooks.com

Contents

Merida's Wild Ride

It was a soggy, stormy afternoon. Merida sat in the stables reading from an old book of Highlands tales. She and her horse, Angus, wanted to go for a ride. If only the weather would clear up . . .

"Look, right there," Merida said. "Magical horses. That one there is called a kelpie. It's a water horse."

Angus snorted, shaking his head. It was clear that he wanted nothing to do with magic, especially after their last encounter.

The raindrops slowed
and the clouds scattered.

"Come, lad," said Merida to Angus. "The sun's breaking through. Let's go for a ride."

They galloped across the bridge and down the hill.

Just as they reached the woods, a flash of gray caught Merida's eye. "What was that?"

But Angus didn't want to follow—whatever it was.

"Don't be a ninny," Merida chided him. "I'm sure it's not a bear."

Merida guided Angus to a clearing. In it stood
a magnificent gray horse. Its coat shimmered. Its
mane was like fine silk.

Breathless with excitement, Merida whispered
to Angus, "I know that horse is magical."

The horse lowered its head as Merida approached.

Suddenly, Angus blocked Merida's path.

"Angus," she called, "don't be jealous, lad! This horse must be lost. We need to help it—make sure it's safe."

Merida talked to the gray horse, and it responded with a soft whinny.

She showed the horse that she was not dangerous, that she was a friend. She was excited to encounter a magical horse.

Merida swung onto its back. She didn't have a bridle, but she knew she could guide the horse with her hands wrapped in its mane. The horse bolted, but Merida wasn't frightened. She had been around horses all her life.

Merida tried to calm the horse. But it ran on. They were headed toward a large loch—a deep, dangerous lake.

Why did it seem as if her hands were stuck in the horse's mane? Were they entangled in its hair?

The horse brushed against a tree, and trapped rainwater fell down on Merida. Effortlessly, one of her hands came free.

Ahead, a bridle hung from a tree. Merida stretched to reach it as they passed, but it was just beyond her fingertips. "Angus, help! The bridle!" she called.

Merida could only hope that her friend had heard her cry. There was a cliff ahead, between them and the loch. *It'll stop before we get to the cliff,* Merida thought. *Won't it?*

Merida tugged on the horse's mane. It didn't work. She even tried to slide off its side. But she couldn't move.

Merida looked up at the sound of a whinny. It was Angus. He had galloped up next to them— and he was carrying a bridle!

He tossed it. Merida caught it and slipped it
over the charging gray horse's head. With the
reins in her hand, she guided the horse to a path
that led away from the cliff's edge.

And just as they reached the shore of the loch, the horse finally
slowed to a stop. Merida was no longer stuck. She jumped off.

The stallion stood quietly. Merida looked into its eyes for an answer to what had triggered the horse's behavior. Something sparked her memory, and she removed the bridle. The horse's head moved softly as if it were nodding before it galloped down the misty shoreline along the loch.

Merida frowned as she watched the horse. Was it really racing into the water, or was the fog playing tricks on her eyes?

Back at the stable, Merida looked at the book she had been reading. She found the legend of the kelpie. "'Once a bridle is put on a kelpie, the water horse will do your bidding,'" she read.

She looked up at Angus. Was it possible? Had she been riding a kelpie? Either way, Merida would never forget her wild ride!

Princess Polo Games

One morning during breakfast, Jasmine received a letter from the Princess Polo Club.

Dear Princess Jasmine,

Congratulations! You have been selected as a Princess Polo Club team captain.

Please report to Qamar Field tomorrow morning to meet your team: THE ROYAL RAIDERS.

Jasmine wanted to win the Princess Polo Club's golden trophy, just as her mother had many years earlier.

The next morning, Jasmine flew to Qamar Field.

"Welcome, captains!" the chairwoman of the Princess Polo Club said. "Today you will meet your teams. Train them well. At the end of our season, a final match will determine who wins the golden trophy."

"That will be me," said Princess Farah, raising a finger. "I always win, no matter what."

The chairwoman announced the names and members of each team: the Super Sultans, the Majestic Monarchs, the Awesome Aces, and the Royal Raiders.

Jasmine couldn't wait to meet her team: the Royal Raiders!

Princess Farah sniffed. "More like the Royal *Afraiders*."

Jasmine believed in her team—at first.

But one teammate, Kamali, wouldn't let go of her horse's mane; another, Amira, had her nose in a book. And Zayna was doing a handstand. They wouldn't even hold their mallets! Jasmine's hopes for the golden trophy started to fade.

Jasmine went to the chairwoman and said, "There has to be some mistake."

The chairwoman shook her head. "Teams were chosen specifically for each captain's skills. You can do this, Princess Jasmine."

The next day, Jasmine taught her team how to play polo. She showed them how to hit the ball into the goal and how to stop the other team by bumping their horses or hooking their mallets.

The Royal Raiders finished practice at the same time as the Majestic Monarchs.

"Practice was kind of boring," Zayna said, yawning.

"At least your captain seems nice," said a Monarchs player. "Farah is so mean. I thought polo was supposed to be fun."

The next day at practice, Jasmine saw that Kamali was so stubborn about staying on her horse that she could be used to bump into other players to stop them from scoring.

Amira was an amazing scorer—especially when she pretended to be a hero from one of her books.

Once Zayna realized her horse was as energetic as she was, they made a great team— with incredible speed. They always got to the ball first.

Jasmine used the strengths of her teammates effectively to win games. Soon they made it all the way to the finals.

On the day of the finals, Jasmine and the Royal Raiders were facing Farah and her Majestic Monarchs in the final match.

"Well, if it isn't the scaredy-cat, the bookworm, and the jumping bean," said Farah. "Get ready to lose!"

Jasmine huddled with her team moments before the first chukker, or game period. "Farah doesn't know that the very things she teases you about are the things that make you special. Now let's get out there and have fun!"

The game began with Zayna beating Farah to
the ball! The Royal Raiders got the first possession.

In the second chukker, Kamali stopped Farah from scoring not once, not twice, but three times!

Amira scored two goals all by herself in the third chukker. One of them was from all the way across the field!

After the fourth chukker,
the captains rallied
their teams.

"You're doing a great job!"
exclaimed Jasmine. "The score
is tied. We can win this!"

But the Majestic Monarchs weren't
excited. Farah never passed the ball.

In the last chukker, Farah scored to break the tie. The Majestic
Monarchs were up by one. If the Royal Raiders didn't make a goal,
they would lose.

Jasmine prepared to race down the field to score another goal.
But then she saw the Majestic Monarchs players and had an idea. She
called a time-out to talk to her team. Jasmine wanted to keep giving
the other girls a chance to play and have fun.

When the Royal Raiders returned to the field, Jasmine passed the ball—straight to one of the opposing Monarchs players! Kamali and Amira blocked Farah from intercepting a pass to her own teammate, and Zayna cheered the Monarchs all the way down the field. Jasmine's plan was playing out perfectly!

During that last chukker, each Monarchs player was able to score a goal!

The game was over. The Monarchs had won.

Jasmine was glad that everyone on both teams had had a chance to play and have fun. That was more important than winning.

"Congratulations to the Monarchs," said the chairwoman. "The medals go to the winners. But the golden trophy belongs to the most honorable player. This year it goes to . . .

. . . Princess Jasmine!"

"You are a true leader," said the chairwoman, "just like your mother."

Jasmine gasped. "You knew my mother?"

The chairwoman smiled. "Your mother was my team captain."

The Enchanted Unicorn Adventure

Briar Rose—which is what Aurora was known as when she lived with the good fairies—was learning how to plant a garden with her aunts. For weeks they had tended to the seeds, watering, weeding, and *waiting*.

"Oh, won't they hurry up?" Merryweather said. She was ready to see those blooms.

"It'll be worth the wait," Briar Rose said.

But Merryweather didn't like waiting. Later that night, she approached the other fairies.

"You know what would make the flowers bloom?" she whispered to Fauna. "Magic!"

"Oh, for goodness' sake," Flora muttered. In a huff, she went to the cabinet where the magic wands were hidden. "No wands," she said. "We promised."

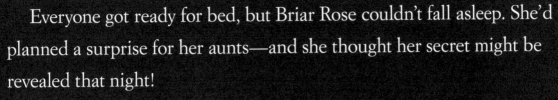

Everyone got ready for bed, but Briar Rose couldn't fall asleep. She'd planned a surprise for her aunts—and she thought her secret might be revealed that night!

"They're blooming!" Briar Rose cried as she dashed down the stairs and out the front door.

"But how could that be?" Fauna asked.

"The sun has already set," Flora replied. Then she gave Merryweather a stern look.

"It wasn't me!" Merryweather cried.

Sure enough, the garden was bursting with blooms.

"Surprise!" Briar Rose shouted. "We planted evening primrose, moonflower, and—"

"Night-blooming flowers!" Fauna interjected. "I should have known!"

Just then, a branch snapped. Briar Rose turned and couldn't believe her eyes.

In the corner of the garden, a family of unicorns was grazing on the moonlit blooms! The baby's horn glittered. Briar Rose's eyes were glued to the magical creatures.

"Unicorns only come out at night—for fear of being seen," Flora said to Briar Rose. "They're shy but friendly, and they must have smelled the flowers. They eat petals."

"What if we don't have enough for them?" Briar Rose asked.

"Don't worry," Fauna said. "There's plenty in this garden. It's a feast!"

Briar Rose couldn't help herself: she had to get closer to those unicorns. So she plucked a flower and offered it to the baby unicorn. The animal was nervous at first, but then it slowly took the flower from Briar Rose. The baby smiled as it ate and then licked Briar Rose's hand as if to ask for more. It tickled!

"You can eat as much as you want," Briar Rose said. "You're safe here."

The fairies enjoyed seeing Briar Rose so happy but sensed their presence was making the unicorn parents a bit uneasy.

"We should let them be," Merryweather suggested. So Briar Rose and her aunts headed back inside.

Meanwhile, Maleficent's raven was out for a night flight. The evil fairy had tasked him with scanning the surrounding area every evening. Most of the time, there was little to report. But that night, he spotted the unicorns, which were very unusual. He immediately returned to Maleficent.

Back in her castle, Maleficent was not pleased.

"Unicorns? In that pesky cottage garden? We'll have to do something about that," she said. Maleficent didn't like anything out of the ordinary, and unicorns were the most extraordinary creatures of all. "When I'm through, no one will be able to enjoy those flowers."

Moments later, a flurry of frost flooded from Maleficent's tower. It moved fast, heading straight for Briar Rose's garden.

"Those unicorns will have a hard time finding something to eat now," the evil fairy said.

Maleficent cackled. She was delighted to have ruined the flowers. She knew it wouldn't be long before the unicorns had no choice but to leave the forest.

Early the next morning, Briar Rose rushed to the garden. But her excitement quickly turned to confusion.

"Frost!" she cried. "What bad luck!"

Briar Rose feared the frost had killed her flowers, thereby leaving her unicorn friends without food. She knew she had to help, so she grabbed her cloak and a basket, then walked into the forest. *Perhaps some flowers are blooming elsewhere,* she thought. She noticed that the frost hadn't traveled far.

She walked for a long time.
Then Briar Rose caught a glimpse
of something moving. For a
moment, she was distracted
from her quest.
*What could
that be?* she
wondered.

It was the
mother unicorn!

"Why, hello there,"
Briar Rose said, relieved.

The mother unicorn had been chomping on a patch of wildflowers.

"Are you trying to bring back food for the baby?" Briar Rose asked.
The unicorn whinnied.

"Let me help," Briar Rose said. And together they plucked an entire
bouquet.

When Briar Rose returned to the cottage, she put the remaining
wildflowers in a vase—just in case the unicorn family stopped by for a
snack.

The next morning, Briar Rose checked on her bouquet, but the flowers were already wilting. "I didn't let frost stop me, and I won't let wilted wildflowers stop me, either," she said. "There must be some flowers that are as strong as I am."

She found her answer in a gardening book. "There *are* flowers that bloom even when it's cold and snowy. In fact, they sometimes bloom best after a frost!"

"Did we plant any?" Merryweather asked.

"We did," Briar Rose answered. "Forget-me-nots. With a little help, they'll be ready by nightfall."

Briar Rose and her aunts spent the whole day tending to the garden. First Briar Rose and Merryweather carefully watered the plants to clear and melt the frost.

Later in the afternoon, Fauna pruned the dead leaves while Flora gathered the debris and cleared it away.

By nightfall, the garden was good as new. And peeking through was a burst of dainty flowers. The sun had set, and the forget-me-nots had blossomed!

Just then, the baby unicorn trotted forward and sniffed the petals.
It started eating, and Briar Rose patted the creature's head.

"I can't believe I have enchanted friends to visit with every night!"
Briar Rose said.

Flora gave the other fairies a sideways glance. "My dear," she began, "as you know, flowers only last for a season."

"I'm afraid unicorns are similar," Merryweather added. "They don't stay in one place for long."

"But maybe they'll be back next year," Fauna said, "like the flowers."

As her aunts wrapped her in a warm hug, Briar Rose was certain of one thing: she could work through any obstacle that was thrown her way—especially with the help of her family.

Snow White's Forest Journey

Snow White and her prince spent nearly every day together. But one particularly sunny morning, the Prince told Snow White that he had an important errand to take care of. "I will be away for several hours, I'm afraid," he said.

"I'll miss you," said Snow White. She herself was planning on spending the day in the palace gardens.

Snow White changed her dress and set about her gardening. The Prince saddled his trusty steed, Astor, and rode to the garden to bid Snow White farewell.

"Take good care of my prince," Snow White said, slipping a flower into Astor's bridle.

Then she gave one to the Prince. "And take good care of Astor!" she said, for Snow White loved the faithful horse, too. She smiled and waved as she watched them trot down the road.

The time flew by. Before long, Snow White looked up from the roses she was tending and saw a cloud of dust on the road. A horse was rapidly approaching.

"Oh, good!" she exclaimed, clapping her hands together. "The Prince and Astor are home early!"

Brushing the dirt from her clothes, she hurried toward the gate to greet them as they arrived.

But Astor was alone! The princess ran down to meet the horse.

"Why, where's the Prince?" she wondered out loud. Her tender heart quickly filled with dread. Surely the Prince was in some sort of trouble.

"I must go find him!" she declared. And without wasting another moment, she grabbed her cloak and started down the road.

The horse stamped her hoof on the ground and nodded toward her empty saddle.

"Do you want me to get on?" Snow White asked. Again, Astor nodded.

Goodness! thought Snow White. *Maybe she can show me where the Prince is!* Quickly, the princess pulled herself into the saddle. She barely had time to sit down before Astor was racing down the road toward the forest.

Astor ran deeper and deeper into the woods, with Snow White tugging uselessly at the reins. The princess tried not to think about what dangers might await them on the dark path ahead.

If only she knew where Astor was taking her . . .

If only she knew that the Prince was safe . . .

Tirelessly, Astor galloped through the woods. She darted between trees and leaped over briars and brambles.

Then, suddenly, Snow White spotted a piece of red cloth caught on a long, sharp thorn.

A knot formed in her throat. Could it be? It was! The cloth was a scrap torn from the Prince's riding cloak!

Astor continued galloping through the forest.

At last, they reached the river. *Surely Astor will have to stop here,* Snow White thought. But the horse's pace only quickened. Indeed, it was soon clear to Snow White that Astor planned to jump across the river!

Suddenly, Snow White saw the Prince's feathered hat dangling from a limb high above the water.

There was no time to think. As Astor leaped across the river, Snow White reached up as high as she could . . . and plucked the hat from the branch.

Snow White gripped Astor's reins with one hand. With the other, she clutched the Prince's hat to her chest. She could only imagine the horrible danger her dear, sweet prince was in.

Her thoughts were soon interrupted by a startling noise.

"Well, tello hair . . . I mean, hello there!" said someone with a familiar voice.

"Doc?" Snow White said with a sigh of relief. "I'm so very glad to see you!"

"Likewise, my dear. But what's the matter?" Doc asked.

"It's the Prince," Snow White said, showing him the crumpled hat. "I have to find him!"

"Don't worry, Princess. We can help you!" Doc assured her.

Doc put his fingers to his lips and whistled. Within seconds, the other Dwarfs arrived.

"The Prince is missin'," Doc explained to the Dwarfs. "And we're gonna help Snow White find him!"

"Let's . . . let's . . . let's—*achoo!*—let's go!" Sneezy cried.

"Oh, thank you," Snow White said as Astor impatiently stamped her hooves. "Just follow Astor," she added. "She seems to know the way."

The Seven Dwarfs and their ponies followed Snow White and
Astor through the depths of the forest and over a deep, rocky canyon.

"Ooh," said Bashful, looking down, "I hope the Prince isn't down
there."

"Shhh! You'll scare the princess," Grumpy growled back at him.

But Snow White had heard. She clutched the Prince's hat and
concentrated on thinking hopeful thoughts.

Finally, they emerged into a sunny clearing, and Astor
slowed to a stop. Snow White blinked in the bright light and
then spotted the Prince lying on the ground. "Oh, no!" she cried.

Astor knelt down slightly so the princess could slip out of the
saddle. The faithful horse whinnied as Snow White ran toward
the Prince.

"Don't worry!" Snow White called to the Prince as she raced across the clearing. "I'm coming!"

She ran as fast as she could, avoiding rocks and twigs on her way to the Prince's side. Was he hurt?

Breathless, Snow White reached the Prince just as he sat up and stretched. "What a nice nap!" he said. "And what a lovely way to awake. I hope you're hungry!"

Snow White was bewildered. Next to the Prince lay a lavish picnic spread out on a soft blanket. And the Prince was as happy and healthy as ever!

"I knew Astor would get you here quickly," he said, beaming. "Tell me: are you surprised?"

Snow White paused for a moment to catch her breath.

"Oh, yes, very surprised," she said at last.

The Prince looked amused as the Seven Dwarfs began digging into the delicious food.

"Well," he said with a laugh, "I'm glad I brought a little extra."

"Me too," Snow White replied. She picked up an apple and offered it to Astor. "And," she added, "I'm very glad you have such a dear and clever horse!"

Aurora and the Joust

Aurora loved being a princess. But after spending so much time in a quiet cottage, her life at the castle was often a bit overwhelming.

One day Aurora was embellishing a flag for the upcoming joust. Soon the whole kingdom would gather to watch knights compete on horseback.

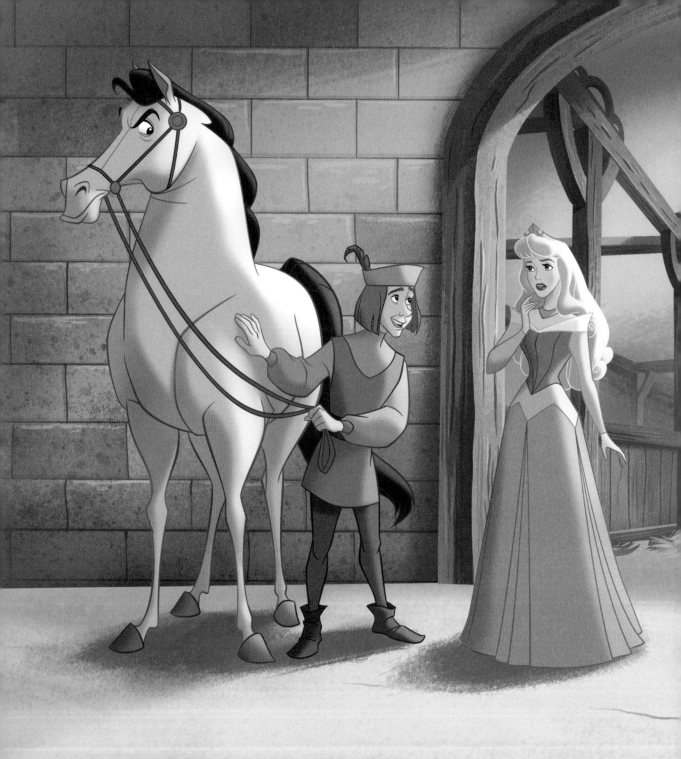

Later Aurora noticed Samson—Prince Phillip's horse—was refusing
to follow the stable hand into his stall.

Aurora rushed to investigate.

"What seems to be the matter?" she asked.

"Samson's just a bit restless," the stable hand explained.

"The prince is traveling, so the horse won't get to compete in the joust," he continued.

"It seems like we both could use some fresh air," Aurora said to Samson. "I'd like to take you somewhere special."

But it was an awkward ride into town.
Samson and Aurora had trouble finding a rhythm.

Eventually, they reached the village.
It was bustling! And the hard feelings
between the new friends started to
melt away.

As they walked, Aurora and Samson got a
closer look at village life.

The carpenter and other locals
were constructing the grandstands
for the tournament.

The blacksmith was forging a helmet for a knight.

Just then, Aurora had an idea.

"What if we compete in the joust together?" she whispered to Samson.

Samson was overjoyed! He immediately raced to
the field where he and Prince Phillip used to practice.
"You are amazing!" Aurora exclaimed. "Is this
where you learned how to joust?" Samson
whinnied loudly in reply.

The tournament was in one week, and there was so much to learn.

In the joust, Aurora would have three challenges.

She had to thread her lance through a series of rings.

She needed to charge at her opponent.

And she had to disarm the knight
pitted against her.

Practicing all three
was fun. But for Aurora,
spending time with Samson was the highlight of each afternoon.

The night before the tournament, Aurora revealed her plan to her
parents. "Since Prince Phillip won't be present for the joust tomorrow,
I'd like to compete in his place."

Her father was nervous. "That seems dangerous," he replied.

After a brief silence, her mother spoke. "You're a new kind of
princess," she said. "It would be our honor to have you participate."

Early the next morning, the townspeople gathered around the jousting arena.

Aurora and Samson took their place among
the competitors. Their hearts raced.

"No matter what happens," Aurora whispered
to Samson, "we are a team."

All of a sudden, their names were
announced. It was time to compete!

Samson took off. Aurora lifted her lance and put it through all the
rings on their path!

Next Aurora and Samson charged toward their opponent—the valiant Sir Kaspar from the kingdom of Blumenfeld.

Finally, Aurora needed to disarm Sir Kaspar. With her lance sturdy in her hand, she tried her best to win this last trial. But their weapons kept getting locked. She needed to try a different tactic.

As Aurora was thinking, Sir Kaspar sent her lance flying through the air!

With her weapon gone, Aurora and Samson were defeated.

At the end of the day, the winners were announced. Aurora and Samson had finished in fourth place!

"Not bad for our first tournament," Aurora said. She and Samson made an amazing team!

Bedtime for Max

It was a beautiful morning in the kingdom. Everyone was enjoying the day—everyone, that is, except the captain of the guard, Maximus. Max was hard at work, patrolling the streets for troublemakers and evildoers.

"Is it just me, or does Max look . . . strange?" Eugene asked Rapunzel as they strolled through town.

Rapunzel studied Max. He had dark circles under his eyes, and his normally neat mane was messy. "You're right," she said. "He looks like he hasn't slept in weeks!" Eugene and Rapunzel found Max's second-in-command and asked him what was wrong with their friend.

"The captain has been so worried about doing a good job," the
guard said, "that he hasn't been sleeping. No matter how many guards
we put on duty, he insists that *he* needs to stay on patrol!"

Rapunzel was worried. Refusing to sleep couldn't be good for Max.
"You know what this means," she told Eugene with a knowing look.

"Plan time?" Eugene asked.

"Plan time," Rapunzel agreed.

The two went off to figure out their plan. When they returned, they found Max running drills with his guards.

"Max!" Rapunzel cried. "I can't find Pascal anywhere! Can you help me find him? I'm afraid something might have happened!"

Max puffed out his chest. He was on the case! He started to sniff the ground, searching for the chameleon's scent.

Eugene and Rapunzel followed Max all around town.

"Can you smell him?" Rapunzel asked.

Max sniffed around all the carts, leading Rapunzel and Eugene this way and that. They checked all Pascal's usual hiding places. But he was nowhere to be found.

Finally, as they turned toward the stables, Max caught the chameleon's scent.

The friends burst through the stable doors, eager to rescue Pascal. But he was fast asleep on a pile of hay!

"You found him! Great job, Max!" Rapunzel said.

"Say, Max, ol' buddy," Eugene said, "since we're here, in the stables, with this nice pile of hay, what do you say to a nap?"

But Max just shook his head. He was too busy to take a break!

Rapunzel and Eugene looked at each other, disappointed. They had hoped that by tricking Max into following them to the stables, they could convince him to rest. But it looked like they were going to need another plan. Luckily, Eugene was on the case!

A little while later, Eugene and Rapunzel found Max inspecting ships that had just arrived at the harbor.

"Max! All the apples have been stolen from the orchard!" Eugene shouted.

Max knew he had to do something. He couldn't let a thief get away on his watch! He raced toward the apple orchard with his friends close behind.

Together, the team searched the orchard for clues about the missing apples. Soon Max spotted some footprints. He and his friends followed them back to the palace and into the kitchen . . . where they found a piping hot apple pie!

The apples hadn't been stolen after all. The chef had used them to make a special treat for the royal family's dinner.

"Apple pie! I love apple pie!" Eugene exclaimed. "But it always makes me sleepy. Do you want a bite, Max?"

But Max just shook his head again. He didn't have time for pie! With the case of the missing apples solved, he had to get back to work. The kingdom needed him!

Disappointed, Eugene looked at Rapunzel. He had been sure that his plan was going to work!

"Maybe we can tire him out enough that he has to sleep?" Rapunzel suggested. "We just need to make him run around for a while." Suddenly, she had an idea.

"We have to go to the Snuggly Duckling!" Rapunzel told Max. "The pub thugs are in trouble!"

Trouble was the only word Max needed to hear. He motioned for Rapunzel and Eugene to hop on his back, and the three galloped toward the Snuggly Duckling.

Max burst into the Snuggly Duckling. He scanned the tavern, looking for the troublemakers. But everyone was gathered around the piano, singing and laughing.

Max looked suspiciously at Rapunzel and Eugene. No one was in trouble! With a sigh, he turned to leave.

"Wait, Max," Rapunzel said. "We're sorry we lied to you. We were just worried. The truth is we've been trying all day to make you rest."

"We were just trying to help," Eugene added.

"You *do* need a break, Max," Rapunzel said. "Can't you just stay for one song?"

Max was touched that his friends cared enough to spend the day trying to help him. With a whinny, he agreed. One song couldn't hurt.

The three friends got ready to listen to the music. Rapunzel hopped away to the piano. Max looked around one last time to make sure that no one was really in trouble.

Rapunzel grinned and whispered something in Hook Hand's ear. He nodded and then began to play a quiet, peaceful lullaby on the piano.

As Rapunzel sang along, she noticed Max swaying to the music. Slowly, his eyes began to close. Soon Max was fast asleep.

Eugene put a blanket over Max, and Rapunzel motioned for
everyone to quickly leave the Snuggly Duckling. As the thugs quietly
closed the door behind them, Rapunzel gave Eugene a hug. They all
watched as Max snoozed away. He looked so peaceful. The thugs gave
a soft *aww*. It had taken them all day, but they had finally gotten Max
to take a well-deserved break!

Against All Odds

Princess Jasmine and Aladdin were strolling across the palace grounds one evening when the Sultan ran out onto the balcony.

"Drat!" the Sultan cried. "That dratted Desert Race!"

Every year, the best riders from Agrabah competed against the riders from a neighboring kingdom. The fastest horse and rider were awarded a giant golden trophy.

Jasmine's father was upset because the prince of the neighboring kingdom had won it for the previous three years.

"I have an idea, Father!" Jasmine said eagerly. "I could ride my horse Midnight in the Desert Race this year. He's the fastest horse in Agrabah!"

The Sultan wasn't sure. Jasmine had never raced before.

"How about if *I* ride Midnight in the race?" Aladdin suggested. He had participated in many competitions on the streets of Agrabah.

They all agreed Aladdin would compete in the race.

Nobody but Jasmine had ever ridden Midnight. So the next day, they went to the stables to give Aladdin and the horse a chance to get to know each other.

When Aladdin went toward him with the saddle, Midnight jumped out of reach. When Aladdin swung up onto Midnight's back, the horse kicked up his heels. Aladdin went flying!

But when Jasmine climbed on the saddle, the horse did everything she asked.

It looked like Midnight was a one-princess horse.

Aladdin said he would find another horse to ride in the race.

The day of the race arrived. Riders from the neighboring kingdom paraded into Agrabah, including the prince and his big white stallion.

When it was time for the race, fans jostled for the best views. It seemed everyone but Jasmine was there to watch.

As they took their spot at the starting line, the prince and his horse looked confident.

Suddenly, Aladdin joined the line. He was riding a very strange-looking blue horse.

In fact, it wasn't a horse at all. It was the Genie in disguise!

The Sultan raised his flag. "One, two, three . . ." he called. "And they're off!"

The race was on!

A black horse with a mysterious veiled rider took the lead right away. As soon as they were out of view of the palace, the rider threw off the veil. It was Jasmine!

"I had to prove you were the fastest horse," she whispered to Midnight.

Jasmine raced hard to keep her lead ahead of the other riders.

As the race went on, Jasmine stayed in the lead. But then the prince and his horse started to catch up! They were shocked when they saw the princess. The prince didn't want to lose.

Jasmine urged her horse on, but Midnight couldn't seem to pull away. The prince's horse was big, strong, and *very* fast. Finally, it edged ahead of Midnight.

"Give up now!" the prince shouted.

Jasmine and Midnight weren't going to let the prince and his horse win. Midnight galloped hard and passed them.

"That trophy is Agrabah's!" Jasmine called over her shoulder with a laugh.

But the prince and his horse weren't giving up, either. They stayed right at Midnight's heels . . . until the horses had to jump a ditch that crossed their path.

Midnight sailed over it easily, but the prince's horse skidded to a stop, throwing off its rider!

With the prince and his horse out of the running, it seemed there was nothing keeping Jasmine and Midnight from winning.

But just then, Jasmine heard the sound of hoofbeats right behind her. They were coming up fast!

Jasmine turned back to see who was following her. She gasped. It was Aladdin! And there was something off about his horse.

Soon Aladdin and his mystery horse had caught up, and he and Jasmine were fighting for the lead. Jasmine *really* wanted to prove that Midnight was the fastest horse in the two kingdoms, and that she was the best rider. She pushed Midnight harder and harder.

As they neared the finish line, the two horses were neck and neck. First Midnight would pull ahead a tiny bit, then Aladdin's horse would take over. But neither could keep the lead.

The two horses crossed the finish line at the same time!

As soon as Midnight slowed to a stop, Jasmine jumped off. She gave her tired horse a hug and led him to the water trough for a drink.

Her father ran over. "Excellent work, you two! Jasmine, you are a natural racer!" the Sultan cried, grabbing the trophy and holding it up. "Agrabah is victorious at last! Twice over, in fact!"

Her father was right. Both she and Aladdin had won. She needed to congratulate him—and ask him a question.

She walked over to Aladdin, who was standing with his odd-looking horse.

"Congratulations!" he said when he saw her.

"Same to you," Jasmine replied. "But where in the world did you find yourself such a fast horse?"

Aladdin looked at his horse. Then he looked at his feet. He didn't seem to know what to say.

Just then, the Genie changed from a horse back into his usual form. Jasmine gasped. "Sorry, Princess," the Genie said with a wink. "We were just horsing around!"

When the Sultan realized what Aladdin had done, he frowned. The rules said only a horse-and-rider team could win the trophy. Aladdin and the Genie were disqualified. And that meant . . . Jasmine and Midnight were the winners!

Jasmine patted Midnight proudly. Soon she and Midnight took their spots at the head of the victory parade. She had always known Midnight was fast. But she'd never imagined he was so fast that he could match a genie for speed!

The Perfect Team

One morning, Prince Phillip and Princess Aurora decided to go for a ride. When they got to the royal stable, Aurora looked around. There were so many horses! She didn't know which one to choose.

Then Aurora had an idea. "From now on, I think I'd like to ride the same horse every day," she said.

A big palomino horse caught Aurora's eye. He looked strong and friendly.

The groom brought the horse out to the ring and put him through his paces. The horse marched around as confidently as if he were the king himself. He was amazing!

The groom saddled the horse and helped Aurora up.

Aurora mounted the horse and immediately knew this was the horse for her. She hugged him tightly and was eager to ride.

Then Aurora rode him, and she liked the horse even more. "What's his name?" she asked the groom.

"We call him Brutus, Your Highness," the groom replied.

That would not do! "Brutus" sounded fierce and mean. So Aurora gave her horse a new name that was as nice as he was: Buttercup.

Aurora rode Buttercup all around the castle grounds. When a carriage rumbled past, he stood at attention. When Aurora asked him to jump a stone wall, he cleared it effortlessly. Aurora was thrilled. She had found the perfect horse!

The next day, Aurora decided to ride Buttercup out to the fairies'
cottage so they could meet him. Prince Phillip wanted to saddle up
his horse, Samson, and join her. He didn't like her riding through the
woods alone.

Aurora shook her head. "Don't be silly," she said. "I grew up in these
woods. Besides, I won't be alone. I'll be with Buttercup. We'll take care
of each other!"

Phillip knew Aurora was right. He waved goodbye as Aurora and
Buttercup trotted off.

As Buttercup made his way along the smooth path near the castle,
he was confident and brave. But the moment they entered the woods,
he became a different horse. His steps slowed to a crawl. He looked
nervous. When some of Aurora's woodland friends appeared, Buttercup
tried to spin around and run away.

"There's nothing to be frightened of," Aurora said gently, trying to calm her nervous horse.

Buttercup didn't listen. When they came to a fallen log on the trail, Buttercup refused to step over it. And when Aurora asked him to walk through a forest stream, he snorted and shivered.

By the time she reached the fairies' cottage, Aurora was very worried. How could a horse who was so brave at the palace be so timid in the woods?

Flora, Fauna, and Merryweather oohed and aahed when they saw Aurora's new horse. "He's beautiful, dear," Fauna said.

Aurora sighed. Buttercup *was* beautiful. "I just wish he weren't so afraid," she said sadly.

"I'm sure it will be all right," Flora said, smiling. "You'll just need to be patient with him, that's all."

Merryweather moved closer to get a better look at Buttercup. "What a nice coat he has!" she said. "Though he might look even nicer if his hooves were blue."

She aimed her wand. *Zap!* Just like that, Buttercup's hooves turned blue.

"Don't be silly!" exclaimed Flora. "A horse shouldn't have blue hooves. On the other hand, his coat might look prettier in pink."

Zap! Zap! Zap! Back and forth the fairies went, changing Buttercup from blue to pink to green until it was hard to tell what color he was!

As Aurora watched her new horse change colors, she sighed. *That* didn't seem to frighten him, but a stray leaf fluttering down was as scary as a horse-eating dragon to Buttercup.

Suddenly, Aurora sat up. *That's it!* she realized. As a palace horse, Buttercup was used to people, carriages, and smooth paths. But he had never been deep in the forest before! He wasn't used to other animals, thick branches, rivers, and new noises. No wonder everything scared him!

Aurora didn't want to give up on Buttercup. She decided to help him get over his fear, but first she had to get him back to the castle.

Aurora said goodbye to the fairies and began riding home. She did her best to ignore the way Buttercup jumped at every noise. Helping him be brave was going to be hard. How would she teach him?

Just then, Buttercup stopped so suddenly that Aurora almost fell off. When she looked at the trail ahead, she gasped in horror. An enormous mountain lion was blocking their path!

They were in trouble.

If Buttercup could be frightened by a bunny rabbit, he was certain to panic when facing a mountain lion.

But to Aurora's surprise, Buttercup didn't panic. She could tell that he was still scared, but he stood proudly and puffed himself up. Taking a step forward, he snorted angrily. Then Buttercup struck out at the mountain lion with his front hooves.

Aurora hung on. She was still afraid, but Buttercup had made her feel brave, too. Reaching out, she grabbed a sturdy branch from a nearby tree.

"Leave us alone!" she yelled at the mountain lion, waving the branch. "Or else!"

Buttercup pawed at the ground and snorted fiercely again. When
the mountain lion didn't budge, Buttercup leaped forward and pinned
its tail to the ground with one hoof. Then Aurora rapped the mountain
lion smartly on the nose with her branch.

The mountain lion didn't like that at all. It let out an embarrassed yowl, then yanked its tail free and raced away into the woods.

Aurora was pleased with herself—and her horse. Buttercup had been brave when it counted the most.

As the pair neared the edge of the forest, some butterflies fluttered past them. Buttercup's eyes went wide, and he jumped in terror.

But this time, Aurora just smiled. "You helped me feel brave," she said. "Now I want to help you get past your fear of the forest."

She gently stroked the horse's neck and talked to him in a soft voice. A butterfly fluttered closer and closer . . . and finally landed right on Buttercup's nose.

As the butterfly flapped its wings, Buttercup hardly shook at all. Aurora smiled proudly. The fairies had been right. All he needed was a little patience, understanding, and trust.

"Good boy!" she said, praising her horse. "You know, Buttercup, I think we really do make a perfect team!"

Heart of a Champion

Life at the palace was a dream come true for Cinderella, and she took care to share her good fortune with everyone she loved. This included her dear old horse, Major, who had been her faithful friend since she was a child.

One day, Cinderella was visiting Major in the royal stable when her mouse friends Jaq and Gus ran up to tell her that a messenger had arrived at the palace! Cinderella said goodbye to Major and the other horses and hurried off to hear the news.

Cinderella arrived at the castle just in time to hear the Grand Duke read the invitation aloud: "'Dear King—'" he began.

"That's me!" the King said.

"Quite so," the Grand Duke agreed. "Ahem. 'You and your family are hereby invited to attend this year's annual Royal International Horse Show, to be held exactly one week from today. Please choose one member from your royal household to represent you in the competition.'"

"You know, Father," the Prince spoke up, "there's no finer rider in the kingdom than Cinderella. I think she should represent us."

"Cinderella?" the King said in surprise. He rubbed his chin thoughtfully, then smiled. "That," he declared, "is an excellent idea!"

The next thing Cinderella knew, the King was leading her out of the palace and back to the royal stable.

"Naturally," he told Cinderella, his voice echoing across the stalls, "the finest rider in the kingdom must have the finest horse in the kingdom. I have a stable full of champions, my dear. We'll choose the best of the best, and you can begin training right away. Ah, yes! I can see those blue ribbons already!"

But none of the King's horses was quite right.

"Please wait outside for a moment," Cinderella told the King, the Prince, and the Grand Duke. "I know the perfect horse. You'll see!"

Soon Cinderella came out, leading Major! The old horse was a bit bewildered to find himself on display before the King. The King stared at Cinderella and Major in disbelief.

"What's this?" he demanded.

"Why, 'this' is a horse!" Cinderella replied with a laugh. She rubbed Major's shaggy mane. "The best horse in the kingdom, in fact!"

"My dear," said the King, turning up his nose, "if none of my horses suits your fancy, I can have another hundred champions here by morning."

"Major may be old," said Cinderella, "but he has the heart of a champion!"

And with that, she saddled Major and swung herself up.

"Come on, Major," she said. "Let's show them what you've got."

But the first thing Major did was trip over a nearby water trough. Cinderella flew over Major's head. She landed in the trough with a splash! The other horses whinnied with laughter. Major hung his head.

"Don't worry," Cinderella said to the King, as well as to Major. "By next week, we'll be ready."

Every day for a week, Cinderella and Major trained for hours. But Major kept making mistakes.

No matter how sweetly Cinderella urged him, he missed every jump.

And no matter how firmly she steered him, he always took the wrong turn.

"Oh, Major," Cinderella said, patting his shaggy head, "I know you can do it!"

But no one else was quite so sure—especially not Major!

At last, it was the night before the royal horse show.

"Please don't worry," Cinderella told Major. "You're going to be wonderful. Tomorrow will be fun!"

But Major didn't seem to believe her.

"Did someone say 'fun'?" somebody asked. Cinderella turned around. It was her fairy godmother!

"I overheard your little mouse friends talking," she explained. "They said you needed a miracle. So here I am!"

Cinderella laughed and shook her head. "Oh, that's kind of you," she said. "But we don't need a miracle—just a good night's sleep."

"My dear," her fairy godmother whispered, "*you* know Major can win, and *I* know Major can win, but our friend Major doesn't know it at all. What he needs is a reason to feel confident."

And with that, she raised her magic wand and waved it at Major. To Major's amazement, a glass horseshoe appeared on each of his hooves!

"With these horseshoes, you'll never miss a step," she told Major, sneaking a wink at Cinderella. "And while I'm at it," she added, "bibbidi-bobbidi-boo!" She waved her wand again. Instantly, a golden saddle appeared on Major's back, and Cinderella's simple dress became a beautiful riding habit.

"How can we ever thank you?" asked Cinderella.

"As you said," replied her fairy godmother, "just have fun!"

The next day at the horse show, Cinderella saw more fine horses than she ever had before. They all looked like champions—but so did Major! He held his head up high and stamped his hooves proudly. The King himself could hardly believe that Major was the same horse he'd been watching trip and stumble all week long.

Major cleared every jump with ease and never took an awkward step or a wrong turn. He even managed a graceful little bow at the end. And it was all thanks to the magical glass horseshoes—or so Major thought.

Cinderella knew better, though. The glass horseshoes just gave Major the confidence he needed to show everyone the great horse he had always been.

In the end, there was no question about who belonged in the winner's circle.

"First place goes to Princess Cinderella and Major!" declared the judge.

The Prince took Cinderella's hand and gently kissed it. "I knew you'd win," he told her.

Cinderella smiled at Major. "And I knew *you'd* win," she said.

"You know, I had a special feeling about that horse all along . . ." the King told the Grand Duke.

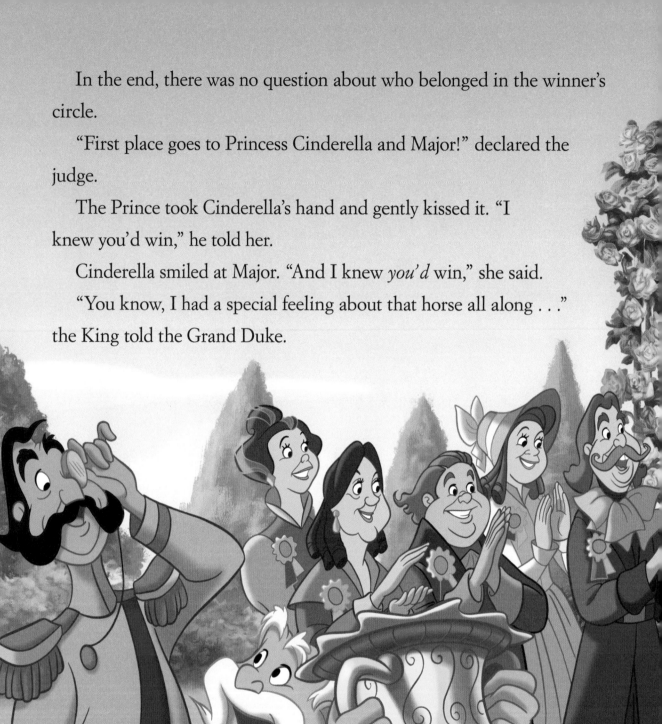

After the horse show, Major returned to his stall at the palace stable with his head a little higher, his back a little straighter, and his glass shoes at the ready for the next time duty called.

A Friend for Philippe

It was a beautiful sunny morning when Belle arrived at Philippe's stable with a special surprise for her friend.

"Guess what I have?" she called happily as she hurried to his stall. "The first carrots of the season, Philippe! I picked them just for you!"

Philippe was not as happy as Belle had hoped he would be. He sniffed at the bunch of carrots. But when Belle offered him one, Philippe gently butted her hand away.

"Is there something wrong?" Belle asked, alarmed. Philippe was always hungry.

Philippe hung his head and sighed a little sigh. There was something wrong, all right, Belle thought. Philippe was the gloomiest horse she had ever seen!

Belle decided that she simply had to cheer up Philippe. But how?

"If only you could talk," Belle said to Philippe, "you could tell me exactly what to do." But he couldn't, so Belle would have to figure it out on her own. She hurried to the library and gathered all the books about horses she could find. Then she sat down to read every single one of them.

But the books didn't hold the answer she was looking for. *I know,* she thought. *I'll ask the Prince what he thinks.*

She found the Prince in his study and explained everything to him. "I wish I knew what Philippe needed!" she cried. "Do you have any suggestions?"

The Prince thought for a moment. "Maybe a walk would do him good," he said. "A good walk always used to cheer me up."

"Of course!" Belle agreed. "That's a wonderful idea!"

Quickly, Belle changed into her riding clothes and hurried to fetch Philippe's saddle. When he saw her coming, he perked right up.

"Silly me! What was I thinking?" Belle said as she saddled him. "You'd *really* like a nice walk, wouldn't you?"

Belle led Philippe to the edge of the forest where the royal orchards began. The sight of all the delicious fruit gave Belle an idea.

"Would you like an apple?" Belle asked. "Go ahead and choose one!"

Following Belle's suggestion, Philippe wandered from tree to tree, eyeing each apple and even sniffing some. But soon his head was hanging, and his steps were slow and heavy. It was clear his heart wasn't in it.

Still, Belle did not give up. They continued to a wide, open meadow.

"You know," Belle said, "I bet a good gallop would do the trick." She leaned forward and snapped the reins, giving Philippe's sides a firm nudge with her heels.

As if to tell her, *Wrong again*, Philippe stopped, leaned down, and nibbled at a clover.

"Oh, Philippe," Belle said in despair. "I just don't know what else to do!"

Then, all of a sudden, Philippe's ears pricked up, and his head snapped to attention. Belle barely had time to sit up before Philippe charged off like a racehorse out of the gate!

"Whoa, boy!" Belle cried, nearly falling out of the saddle. "Philippe! Where are you going?"

But Philippe just charged on, straight into the forest.

At last they emerged from the trees . . . into a clearing filled with beautiful wild horses! Belle and Philippe stared at the herd before them. Then Philippe whinnied, and several of the wild horses answered him. Finally, Belle realized what Philippe had wanted. It wasn't an apple or a run. He had wanted to be with other *horses*!

"Well, go on," Belle said as she swung down and took off Philippe's saddle. "Go have some fun!"

She didn't have to tell him twice. Philippe trotted eagerly over to the herd.

All afternoon, Belle watched Philippe race and play. Soon he had even made a friend! The two horses grazed, chased each other around the clearing, and dozed together in the warm sun.

All too quickly, the day was over, and the sun began to set.

"Oh, goodness!" cried Belle. "We've got to get going!"

So she put Philippe's saddle on and they started back toward the castle. "I promise we'll come back soon!" Belle told Philippe.

As they made their way
through the meadow, Belle
found herself wishing Philippe
had a horse friend at the castle.
Then she heard hooves behind
her and turned around.

"Well, look at that,
Philippe! It's your new friend,"
Belle said.

Belle and Philippe slowed
their pace, and the shy horse
drew closer and closer. By the time they reached the castle, the two
horses were walking side by side.

"Welcome to our castle!" Belle told the new horse when they arrived. "We're honored to have you as our guest!"

And to show the horse she meant it, Belle hurried to fix up the stall next to Philippe's.

"There," she said when she was through. "Now this looks like a stable where a horse—or two—could live happily ever after!"

And that was exactly what they did.

Khan to the Rescue

Mulan sighed loudly as she dipped her brush into the pot of ink and gently touched it to the scroll in front of her. She hated practicing calligraphy. It was so boring.

Outside, she heard a horse neigh in the distance. Mulan wished she was out there, too—not stuck inside with the musty inkpot and her own thoughts.

Ignore it, she told herself. *Calligraphy, calligraphy, calligraphy—*

NEIGH!

Mulan jumped a mile. Her father's horse, Khan, was standing right outside her window!

Mulan hurried outside. Right away she noticed something alarming!

"That's Grandma's hat," Mulan said to Khan. "And that's Grandma's basket. And now, come to think of it, Grandma was going to take you down to the orchard today. And here you are . . ."

But where was Grandma?

Khan pawed the ground impatiently. Mulan knew he wouldn't have left Grandma alone unless she needed help!

Khan whinnied again and tossed his head back toward the saddle.

"You want me to climb up?" Mulan guessed. "You'll take me to her?

"I want to," Mulan told Khan, "but I'm not allowed! Wait here, and I'll run into the village and get help."

Khan butted her urgently with his big soft nose.

"I know," Mulan said, rubbing his ears. Oh, it was so frustrating! Mulan was trying to be a proper lady, and proper ladies did not hop on horses and ride to the rescue.

But maybe just this once . . .

"You're right," Mulan said, making a decision. "There isn't enough time to go to the village."

Just this once.

The moment Mulan settled in the saddle, Khan bolted into a full gallop. He was wasting no time going to rescue Grandmother Fa. The horse raced out of the gate and into the forest.

It was a long way to the orchard. Mulan still didn't know what had happened, but she hoped her grandmother knew that help was coming.

Mulan held on for dear life as the horse sped through the countryside. They galloped over hills and through valleys. They jumped over fallen trees and splashed through rivers.

Soon they arrived at the orchard, and Khan skidded to a stop in front
of the old cherry tree. Mulan slid down from the saddle.

"Grandma?" she called. She looked all around, but she couldn't see
her grandmother. "Grandma!"

"Up here!"

Mulan looked up into the branches of the old cherry tree.

"The ladder fell," Grandma said. "And I couldn't climb down. I'm so
happy to see you, Mulan."

"I'll get you down right away!" Mulan promised. But when she picked up the ladder, it fell apart in her hands.

"Oh, no," Mulan said. "The ladder is broken."

Grandma looked worried. "Maybe you should go get help from the village," she said.

"It would take forever," Mulan replied. "Don't worry, Grandma, I've got this."

Mulan looked around. "Okay," she muttered to herself, "let's see what we have to work with. One horse, one saddle, two baskets, one bridle . . . Aha!" She had the perfect plan.

First she unbuckled Khan's reins from his bridle and tied a piece of her sash to them. Then she tied one end of the leather strap to a basket.

Mulan tossed the strap up to her grandmother. "Sling it over the branch," she instructed. Then she tied the other end of the makeshift rope to Khan's saddle. Mulan held Khan's bridle and backed him slowly away from the tree. The strap tightened, and the basket rose into the air until it was right next to Grandma!

"Step into your chariot, Grandma," Mulan said with a grin. Once her grandmother was safe in the basket, Mulan led Khan forward step by step until the basket was back on the ground.

"You did it!"
Grandma cried,
rushing over to hug
Mulan. "You brave
girl!"

"Well," Mulan said,
blushing. "not *that* brave. I
mean, I wasn't the one stuck
up a tree."

"You *are* brave,"
Grandma said.
"Brave and brilliant."
Mulan and Grandma
took their time
returning home.
Khan didn't
seem to mind—
he paused to
graze as they
went.

"Father will be angry," Mulan told her grandmother nervously. "I was supposed to be practicing my calligraphy today."

Grandma made a thoughtful *hmmm* sound. "I think I can help with that," she said. "Just this once."

That evening at dinner, Mulan's father asked her how her studies had gone.

"Actually," Grandma spoke up, "I helped Mulan with her calligraphy today."

"Oh?" Mulan's father said. He turned to Mulan. "What character did you practice?"

"The character of 'courage,'" she replied. Mulan and Grandma shared a secret smile. "I had a great teacher."

Merida's Winning Friendship

One sunny summer morning, Merida leaped out of bed and threw open the windows. It was the perfect day for the DunBroch Games, a festival held in the spirit of fun and friendship.

Looking outside, she saw clans arriving from across the kingdom. Merida could hardly wait to join the festivities—but first she had chores to do. She had to brush her beloved horse, Angus.

When she had finished her chores, Merida walked out into the sunshine and saw her parents, King Fergus and Queen Elinor. Standing between them was a boy.

"I want you to meet Kendrew," King Fergus said to Merida. "His father is a dear friend from a neighboring clan. I thought you could show him around."

Merida was thrilled. Now she could enjoy the games with someone her own age.

Merida heard cheering from the festival grounds.

"C'mon, Kendrew," she said. "The games are beginning!"

The cheers grew louder as the bagpipers and drummers signaled the start of the games.

Everyone was excited to begin the festivities!

Waving goodbye to her parents, Merida dragged Kendrew away.

Queen Elinor laughed nervously as she watched them go. "Oh, dear. I hope they get along."

But King Fergus wasn't worried. "I'm sure it'll be a winning friendship, my love. Now, which way was the caber toss?"

Merida knew where she wanted to go first—the archery field! Surely Kendrew would like to shoot a few arrows.

Kendrew watched nervously as Merida hit bull's-eye after bull's-eye.

When it was his turn, Kendrew confessed, "I don't have a bow."

"Here," Merida said. "You can borrow mine."

Kendrew smiled at her kindness and reluctantly took the bow.

But Kendrew wasn't the archer Merida was. In fact, he wasn't much of an archer at all.

His arrows hit everything *but* the target. Every time he missed, his face grew sadder.

"That's okay," Merida assured Kendrew. But she felt bad. She had just wanted to find something for them to do together. "What kinds of events *do* you like?"

Instantly, Kendrew perked up. "C'mon, I'll show you!"

Kendrew led Merida toward a group of pipers. He scooped a set of bagpipes into his arms and began playing.

Merida was confused. "But how do you win at bagpipes?" she asked.

"You don't," Kendrew replied. "You just play."

"Here, you try!"
Kendrew said, and
passed the instrument
to Merida.

Holding bagpipes reminded Merida of wrestling her brothers on bath day. When she tried to play a tune . . . what a ruckus!

Kendrew saw that Merida wasn't having any fun. Now *he* felt bad. "Let's go find something else to do," he suggested.

Merida and Kendrew continued to wander through the fairgrounds, but neither was having much fun.

It seemed whatever she liked, he didn't . . .

and whatever he enjoyed, she didn't.

Merida wondered if there was anything she and Kendrew
could enjoy together.

Just then, they came to the last tent at the festival. They stopped in front of a sign that read PET COSTUME CONTEST.

Kendrew sighed. "I've always wanted to enter this contest. I love to sew, but I don't have a pet to make a costume for."

Suddenly, Merida had an idea.

Merida told Kendrew
to wait for her and
hurried off. When
she returned, Merida
wasn't alone. She had
brought Angus!

"He's perfect!" Kendrew exclaimed.

Merida was happy. Maybe this was something they both could do.

Together, they set to work. While
Merida schemed, Kendrew sewed.

While Kendrew
cut, Merida calmed.

While Merida
wiggled, Kendrew
wobbled.

Working together, they created an outfit like nothing else that had ever been seen (or worn) by man or beast.

When the contest was over, Merida and Kendrew had taken first prize!

"You were right, dear," said Queen Elinor to King Fergus, watching as the new friends rode off on Angus. "It was a winning friendship after all!"